SOCCER
STAND-OFF

BY JAKE MADDOX

text by
Eric Stevens

STONE ARCH BOOKS
a capstone imprint

Jake Maddox JV books are published by
Stone Arch Books
A Capstone imprint
1710 Roe Crest Drive
North Mankato, Minnesota 56003
www.mycapstone.com

Library of Congress Cataloging-in-Publication Data is available on the
Library of Congress website.

ISBN: 978-1-4965-3983-0 (hardcover) 978-1-4965-3987-8 (paperback)
978-1-4965-3991-5 (ebook PDF)

Summary: Ethan is devastated when his soccer coach leaves the team, but is even more alarmed when the new coach is his dreaded biology teacher, Ms. B. Ethan must decided whether or not he will try hard to improve his soccer or continue blaming everyone else for his nonstarting position.

Art Director: Nathan Gassman
Designer: Sarah Bennett
Production Specialist: Katy LaVigne

Photo Credits:
Shutterstock: Aaron Amat, design element, Brocreative, design element, DeanHarty, design element, Eduard Kyslynskyy, design element, hin255, design element, irin-k, design element, Shawn Pecor, Cover

Printed and bound in the United States of America.
009622F16

TABLE OF CONTENTS

CHAPTER 1

SOCCER COACH DISASTER

Ethan rode down the sidewalk on his bike, eager to meet his best friend. He turned onto 23rd Avenue and caught a glimpse of Malik as he rose from the stoop on the corner. Ethan and Malik had played together on the Madison Middle School soccer team last year when they were in seventh grade. Now as eighth graders they'd probably be starters. Ethan felt a burst of nerves thinking about their first practice being held today.

Based on the first few practices, the coach would decide who started and at what position. Even though Ethan was pretty much a shoo-in, it was still nerve racking.

Up ahead, Malik waved as he walked his bike to the sidewalk and climbed on. "Hey, Ethan!" he yelled. "You ready?"

Ethan rolled to a stop next to his friend. "You know it," he said, putting his hand out for a high five. "Good summer?"

"Not bad," Malik said. "Got home last night."

Malik had spent the last four weeks of summer in Alaska with his sister. She lived on an organic farm as a researcher, studying something Ethan didn't understand.

"How about you?" Malik asked as the boys started pedaling toward the school.

"Are you kidding?" Ethan said, shaking his head. "I've been so bored. With you and Jake out of town, I had nothing to do!"

The boys' other best friend, Jacob Levy, had been away almost the whole summer, too. His mom had a temporary assignment in California for work and the whole family went along. Ethan had heard almost nothing from him all summer.

A few more minutes of pedaling and the school came into view. Just as they pulled up, the phone in Ethan's pocket vibrated. "It's a text from Jake," he said, looking at the screen. "He says, 'We need to talk right now.'"

"Right now?" Malik said as he locked up his bike. "Shouldn't he be here, too?"

"Good point," Ethan said. He typed quickly back to Jake: *First practice is starting. Where are you?* Then he locked up his bike and jogged to the field with Malik. The rest of the team was already there, kicking the ball around.

"Hey, Jake's dad's not here either," Malik said as he pulled a ball from the yellow netted sack and tossed it to Ethan.

Ethan coolly caught the ball with his foot and started juggling it. He showed off sometimes, but he couldn't help it. He hadn't even had to practice to get good at juggling. Might as well show off.

Ethan spotted Jerome Grouse from last year's team stretching at the fence. He dribbled over to him. "Hey, where's Coach Levy?"

"I don't know, man," Jerome said, jogging in place.

Just then, a whistle blew from the hill overlooking the field, halfway between them and the rear entrance to the middle school. Ethan looked up and saw a shadowed figure standing at the top, the rising sun behind it.

He quickly pulled out his phone and furiously texted Jacob again: *What the heck is going on? Where are you and your dad?*

The figure at the top of the hill walked toward them, and as Ethan began to make out the face and clothes, dread flooded through him.

"No . . . ," he said quietly, to no one in particular.

The person coming down the hill was Ms. Brezinka, the coach of the girls' soccer team — and his horrible seventh grade science teacher.

Seventh grade science: the class Ethan barely squeaked through with a D the year before, and only after an extension into July to re-do failed labs and exams. He and two other students had been alone in the science room with Ms. Brezinka for four weeks. He'd never spent so much time with one teacher in his life.

Ms. Brezinka stopped and blew her whistle, her clipboard cradled in one arm and her mouth set in a wicked-looking frown. The boys looked at each other and then walked over, Ethan in particular dragging his feet.

"Good morning, Muskrats," she said, looking over the assembled group of soccer players. "My name is Coach Brezinka, and I'm your new coach.

You may know me from the girls' team or from science class."

"Um," Ethan said, casually raising one hand and forcing a smile, "you mean for today? Till Coach Levy gets back from Cali, right?"

"With any luck, Coach Levy will find a new team on the West Coast to work with," she said. "But I got an urgent phone call this morning from the principal looking for a replacement. She was in quite a panic. So now here I am."

Ethan's phone vibrated in his hand. It was Jake again: *Last minute family decision. Mom's taking a permanent transfer. We're staying in Cali.*

"Oh, no," Ethan whispered to himself. *Ms. Brezinka's going to be our permanent coach!*

"Sorry, bro," Malik said quietly next to him, patting him on the shoulder. He knew how hard the science class had been for Ethan. "It's going to be a tough season for you."

CHAPTER 2

TRYING TRYOUTS

"Man, this stinks," Ethan said.

He and Malik leaned against the fence and took long drinks from their water bottles. They ran drills for the first half of practice. After a quick break and some shifting of orange cones, they'd have a scrimmage.

Ethan, though, had trouble in the drills. The shock of seeing Ms. B. still sat in Ethan's mind like a stone. Her presence slowed him down and numbed his reflexes.

Malik nodded. "Jake should be keeper this year," he said. "He could have been starting keeper last year, if you ask me."

"No doubt," Ethan agreed. "And his dad was a great coach. Now we're stuck with this demon woman."

Malik laughed. "Mr. Levy would probably have been coaching the high school team — varsity — if not for Jake being on the middle school team."

"He would have moved to the high school team next year, I bet," Ethan said, pushing off the fence and grabbing his ankle to stretch the muscles in his thigh. "But I'm talking about Ms. Brezinka."

"Ah, don't worry about that," Malik said. "I don't think you stinking at science will matter when she's your coach."

"Man, I'm not worried about that," Ethan said, irritated. Why would Malik immediately think that? "I'm talking about how I don't think Ms. Brezinka knows the first thing about coaching soccer."

"She ran the drills all right," Malik pointed out.

Ethan waved off the idea. "You can get those off any website."

A little farther along the fence, well out of earshot of the rest of the team and Ms. Brezinka, a couple of other eighth graders talked close together, thick as thieves. Ethan strode over to one of them, Conner Stone.

"Bro," Ethan said quietly. "You guys talking about Ms. B.?"

"Yeah," Conner said. "I don't think the girls' team *girl* coach can coach our team."

Ethan considered that and then nodded enthusiastically. "I know! What should we do?"

Conner shared a look with Henry and Philip, standing next to him. "We're leaving," he said. "I already called my dad. He says he'll pay for me to join the Eagles' camp."

The Eagles were the local pro team. They had training camps for youth players all year round.

Ethan thought about it. He was pretty sure his dad wouldn't pay the camp fees — especially for this reason — but he couldn't stand the thought of being coached by Ms. Brezinka.

"Wow, you guys are really going to quit the team?" Malik said quietly. Ethan hadn't even heard him come up. "Isn't that a little extreme?"

"We're pretty extreme," Philip said. Henry laughed.

"Man, I'm angry," Conner said, furrowing his brow. "Since when is the boys' team second-class? Like, we don't even deserve to have a real coach? This is bull."

Ethan felt a little uncomfortable with that. He hadn't thought of it that way. Still, Ms. B. *was* the worst.

Conner turned to Henry and Philip. "Let's go."

"You're not even going to finish practice?" Malik said. They ignored him and started walking away.

Ethan watched them go. He checked on Ms. B. She was clear across the field placing a cone in the corner kick area.

Malik stood beside him, watching intently. "They're full of it, man," Malik said. "She's been the girls' coach for years. I'm sure she knows her stuff."

Ethan whispered back, holding onto Conner's and his friends' idea, "Girls' soccer is a different game. It's not as rough. It's not as athletic."

Malik looked at him sideways. "You've seen a lot of girls' soccer games?"

Ethan shrugged. "I mean. They're girls." Another pang of discomfort ran through him. He shook it off.

"And that's all this is about?" Malik asked. "Nothing to do with science class?"

"Don't be ridiculous," Ethan said. The irritation was back. Why did he have to keep bringing up the science class? The one where he'd done so poorly, Ms. B. had to take pity on him and give him extra help. It was humiliating. He wanted to forget it ever happened. He watched as Conner, Henry, and Philip walked through the gate to leave the athletic field. He made a decision.

"Wait up!" he called after them, jogging across the field toward the gate. The three of them stopped at the fence.

But Ms. Brezinka had finished setting up the boundaries for the scrimmage, and she stood at the center spot, her arms crossed, watching the fleeing boys.

She yelled across the athletic field, "Mr. Isaac!"

Ethan stopped short and turned around. Everyone else on the field watched him.

"Giving up already?" she asked. Her eyebrows arched.

"It's not like that," Ethan muttered.

She gave him a look for a few seconds and then added, "Can't say I'm surprised. You seemed to give up in my science class last year, too, when things didn't go the way you thought they would."

Ethan's face burned. That wasn't it. That wasn't it at all. But no way would he let her win this.

"I'm not giving up," he shouted at Ms. B.'s back. She stopped and turned around, a slight smile on her face.

"All right," she said. "Then get back over here and grab a pinny for the scrimmage."

Ethan clenched his jaw and turned to watch as Conner, Philip, and Henry left the field. He knew it was now or never.

But Ms. B.'s words rang in his ear. "Fine," he said, and turned around. He stomped to the field, determined to prove her wrong.

CHAPTER 3

RUNNING DRILLS

The next practice was two days later. Ethan was up early in the morning and sitting at the breakfast table, shoveling cereal into his mouth, when his mom came in.

"You look grumpy," she said. "Aren't you excited for soccer season?"

Ethan shrugged one shoulder. "I was."

"What changed?" she asked, pouring herself a coffee and sitting across from him.

"The Levys moved to California," Ethan said.

"Oh, yeah," Mom said. "Dad mentioned that. That's too bad. I'll miss Jacob's bright personality around here."

Ethan waited a second, not knowing whether or not he should tell his mom. Finally, he couldn't help himself. "The new coach is Ms. Brezinka," he said, not looking her in the eye.

His mom's face lit up. "She's terrific," she said. "She really stuck with you to help you through that science class that gave you so much trouble."

Ethan rolled his eyes. "You mean she tortured me."

"I hardly think giving you extra chances and tutoring you is torture. I think she pushed you and made you work for your grade — she didn't let you get away with things like other teachers have in the past."

His mom's smile made anger shoot all the way through him. Before he could stop himself, he said,

"Whatever. Anyway, she's a girl, Mom. She can't coach the boys' team."

His mom set her coffee cup down, hard. "Excuse me? I don't think we raised you to think like that, thank you very much."

Ethan swallowed. He knew he'd gone too far. But it was too late now — he'd jumped into the fight with both feet. He put his cereal bowl in the sink, his ears burning.

His mom wasn't through. "If you for one second really think that a woman couldn't coach your team, then we have some conversations coming up, young man. Because maybe you haven't noticed, but I'm a girl, too."

Ethan put his hand on the doorknob. A warning light came on in his head. He knew he shouldn't say the thought that had popped up. But his mom seemed so smug about the science class, the class that made him feel dumb and unworthy. He felt the comeback bubble up inside him and then it bubbled over. "Yeah, I know you're a girl. And you can't coach soccer, either." With that, he ran out the door before his mom could yell at him.

* * *

Practice later that day didn't get any better.

It started with a standard soccer drill. "Dribbling, passing, and shooting," Ms. Brezinka explained as the boys formed two lines. "This line will shoot on goal. This line will dribble through the line of cones and pass to the shooter from this line. After you take your shot, go to the back of the passing line. Got it?"

The crowd of boys mumbled in response.

"Excuse me?" Ms. Brezinka said. "And to think everyone warned me the boys' team would be rowdy. I can't hear you. Everyone got it?"

"Yes, Coach!" the boys shouted in reply.

Except Ethan. He could hardly bring himself to open his mouth. But he lined up with the others and got ready to drill. He didn't move very fast, though, so he ended up at the back of the shooting line.

Malik was a few spots ahead of him. When his turn came, the pass wasn't perfect, but Malik hurried up, took control of the ball, dribbled to the right, and fired a nice shot into the upper left corner.

"Nice one, Malik," Ms. Brezinka said. Then she added, "And Preston, get better control of those passes. Assists win games."

Ethan rolled his eyes and gave Preston a high five when he got behind him in line. "Don't worry about her," Ethan said.

Preston shrugged one shoulder. "It was a messy pass."

"Like Ms. B. knows a messy pass," Ethan said. He could practically see his mother's face glaring at him — his dad's too — but he pressed stubbornly on. "Every pass the girls' team makes is probably messy," he muttered.

The line moved fast, and before long Ethan was at the front. He jogged out from the line as Garret, a seventh grader, rolled him an easy pass.

Ethan smoothly snatched the ball and shot a nice lob directly into the middle of the net, barely putting any power behind it.

"Um, Ethan?" Ms. Brezinka said. "You think we'll be playing against empty nets?"

"Pff," Ethan said through his teeth as he jogged to the back of the other line.

"A little hustle, please," Ms. Brezinka called out.

"I'm hustling," Ethan mumbled. "We're all hustling."

If she heard him, Ms. Brezinka ignored the comment and went back to coaching the players taking passes and shots. "Show me some moves, boys," she called out. "Pretend there's a keeper in that goal and fake him out."

When it was Ethan's turn to pass, the shooter was Elan, another eighth grader. Ethan's pass was easy and slow. Elan strolled up to the ball as it slowed to a stop and walloped it into the goal.

"Any defense out of diapers could have blocked that pass, Ethan," Ms. B. said. A few of the boys laughed — including Malik.

"Might be easier to play for real if you put someone in goal, Ms. B.," Ethan called out, grinning for his friends. A few of the boys laughed, but Malik just shook his head.

Ethan ran to the back of the shooting line again.

"You're right, Ethan," Ms. B. said.

As the lines moved along, Ms. B. placed her clipboard on the grass at her feet. She pulled the whistle from her neck and dropped it on top of the clipboard. As Ethan stepped up to be the next shooter, Ms. B. stretched a little and jogged to the open net.

"All right, Ethan," she said. "You've got yourself a keeper. Let's see if you have an easier time playing for real now."

"This should be easy," Ethan said smugly, though he didn't exactly feel it. As Garret passed the ball to him, some nerves fluttered in his stomach. The pass was faster this time and Ethan had to hustle a little to grab it.

He took control, dribbled toward the goal to his right, and then shot left, hoping to catch Ms. B. off guard.

It didn't work.

Ms. Brezinka barely had to try. She took two quick steps to her right and snatched the ball out of the air with her hands. "You're right, Ethan. This is way better."

"All right, all right," Ethan said to the laughs of his teammates as he jogged to the back of the passing line. "I'm still getting warmed up." He could feel his face getting red, and not from any hard work on his part.

"Okay," Ms. B. said, clapping three times. "I'm keeping for the rest of the drill. Ten more minutes, then we break for a scrimmage. Who's going to score on me?"

No one did.

"Still think she doesn't know anything about soccer?" Malik asked after the drill was over and the boys took a quick break for water. For the scrimmage, they split into two teams by first name: A through L, and M through Z.

"She's a grown-up blocking shots from a bunch of kids," Ethan said. "It's not that impressive."

"If you say so," Malik said.

"It's true," Ethan said. The familiar anger shot through him. Ms. B. had clearly brainwashed his best friend. "No one's even trying that hard."

"I tried," Malik said as he tossed his water bottle to the grass and jogged over to grab a red jersey for the scrimmage. "I wanted to be the first one to score against her. I know I'm not the only one. Good luck in the scrimmage."

CHAPTER 4

SCRIMMAGE!

"Boys," Ms. B. said as half the boys pulled on red mesh pinnies. Ethan got to just wear his T-shirt. "Take the position you'd like to play this season — I want to see who is interested in each position."

Lots of guys tried to take forward since almost all of them wanted a chance to score. Ethan was no different. He grabbed the right wing.

"Don't worry if you don't get forward," Ms. B. called, over the din of boys arguing. "We'll switch up later. And hey, we do need great defense, too."

That quieted everyone down and Ethan smiled, happy with the position he managed to snag. The position he belonged in. On the other side of the center line, Malik lined up as left wing, facing Ethan.

Ms. Brezinka placed the ball at the center spot. "Red kicks off," Ms B. said, "to make up for having to wear those things."

A few boys laughed. Ethan rolled his eyes. Ms. B.blew her whistle, and the scrimmage began.

The red team moved the ball quickly down the right side of the field. The action passed by Ethan and he watched as his midfield let the red team through.

"Oh, come on!" Ethan called downfield.

The defense closed in. Malik cut across the penalty arc and took a pass. He kicked the ball into the box as the kid at center — a seventh grader Ethan hardly recognized — moved toward it at just the right time.

"Great pass, Malik!" Ms. B. called from the sideline, but the seventh grader took a weak shot and the keeper made an easy save.

The keeper knocked the ball to midfield and the midfielders had no problem clearing it.

Ethan ran toward the center. The boy at striker drove up the middle and then passed right. Ethan had to sprint to pick up the pass but the red defense moved slowly and he charged unchallenged up the right side.

His eyes moved from the ball to the goal ahead, back to the ball, and then back to the defense, who were still guarding the center.

I got this, Ethan thought as he closed in on the penalty area. But when he got close, the D sprang into action — suddenly, he was surrounded. He spotted his teammate Sam Berger open behind him to the left.

Ethan dropped back. Using his fanciest footwork, he flipped the ball between his feet, throwing his defenders off guard. Then he flicked it backward to Sam.

"Shoot, Sam!" he yelled.

Sam drove at the keeper and fired a shot. Unfortunately the red keeper was right there. The shot practically hit him in the chest and he wrapped his arms around the ball.

"Good shot, Sam," Ethan said as the boys fell back toward the center line. He gave him a high five.

"Think that one over, boys," Ms. B. said from the sideline. "Sam, make sure you keep your eyes on the goal. If the keeper is blocking the angle, pass to someone else for the shot. Jerome was open."

Seriously? Ethan thought to himself. He snorted out loud and slowed down his run. *Is she just going to pick on me the whole day? This is science class all over again. Why even try at all if this is the way it's going to be?*

"All right, let's mix it up," Ms. B. announced. "If you're at offense, slide on back and let the boys on D have a chance."

Shaking his head, Ethan jogged downfield to switch with one of the guys in midfield. He passed Malik as he went.

"She's right, though," Malik said.

"What?" Ethan snapped, spinning to face him.

"Keeper was right in front of Sam," Malik said. "He should've passed. Jerome was right there. "

Ethan didn't reply. He just grabbed right wingback so at least he'd still be up near the goal when his team had the ball.

Ethan never really got a chance to take another shot and in the end, red won the scrimmage with one goal to zero. Still, he didn't really care. He was a third year — he didn't need to prove himself.

"I'll email the roster first thing in the morning," Ms. B. said as the practice broke up. "Including the starting lineup."

Ethan and Malik shared a look. They had to be starters this year. It was a lock, for sure.

On the bike ride home, Ethan was quiet.

"You mad?" Malik asked.

"No," Ethan said, pedaling a little faster.

"Good," Malik said. "I think she's a good coach."

Ethan's face burned. Yeah. He was mad. "That's because you don't know anything about soccer."

Malik laughed. As he stopped in front of his own house and Ethan rode on, Malik called after him, "Yup. Nothing. That's why the red team won today, right?"

Ethan shook his head and kept riding, wondering how everything got so messed up. When he walked in the front door, the look on his mom's face told him things were going to get messier.

CHAPTER 5

ROSTER RAGE

After a stern talking to from his mom and dad, Ethan had managed not to get grounded for smarting off to his mom. So when he woke up the next morning, he was in a pretty good mood as he logged into his email. Sure enough, he had a new message from Ms. Brezinka.

"Whether she likes me or not," he said to himself before he clicked to open it, "it's my third year on the team. She has to put me on the starting lineup."

He laughed and said louder, to no one, "Not to mention I'm one of the best out there."

The email clicked open and expanded. He scanned Ms. B.'s opening paragraph — just stuff about how excited she was for the season and other stuff Ethan didn't care about. Below was an attached document.

Ethan clicked it open and leaned closer to the display.

"Wait . . . what?" he mumbled as he scanned the list of players and positions.

His name was not there. Not there at all.

"Malik's left wing . . . " He scanned again. Nothing.

He grabbed his phone from his desk and typed a text: *M, did she cut me??*

A moment later, his phone vibrated: *Look closer.*

Ethan ran his eyes down the roster. "Isaac, E." was definitely not there.

Look at what? My name's not there.

You're looking at the starting roster, Malik replied. *There are two attachments.*

"What?" Ethan said, closing the roster. Malik was right. At the bottom of Ms. B.'s email was a second document. Ethan double clicked it.

The title was "Madison Middle School Muskrats — Full Roster," and Ethan's name was on that list.

"Second-string fullback?" Ethan said out loud. "I'm not a defender!"

Ethan was furious. He scanned the email again. There was a practice this weekend. He set his jaw and texted Malik: *No way. I'm not letting her do this. Will you have my back this weekend?*

Malik didn't reply. Ethan threw his phone on his bed.

CHAPTER 6

CAPTAIN'S PRACTICE

Saturday morning, Ethan rode alone to the
athletic field at Madison Middle School. He'd been
mad at Malik since Thursday morning, when he
hadn't replied to his text.

Ethan was early and only Jerome was there. He
walked from the equipment shed, dragging the net
bag of soccer balls with one hand and balancing a
stack of orange cones with the other.

"Where's Ms. B.?" Ethan said.

"Didn't you look at the email?" Jerome said. "Captain's practice. Coach Brezinka isn't coming. I'm leading the practice."

"What?" Ethan said. He followed Jerome out to the field.

"I'm the captain and it's captain's practice, so . . . ," Jerome said. He dropped the bag of balls. "You want to help me set up?"

"I mean, that's cool," Ethan said. "I know you can lead a team. You'd be a better coach than Ms. B. any day. But I have to talk to her."

"Emma will be here in a bit," Jerome said. Eighth grader Emma Tzuck was the team manager. She had been for the last two years.

Ethan shook his head. "I have to talk to Ms. B."

"Something wrong?" Jerome asked.

"Yeah, something's wrong," Ethan said. A few other boys arrived, some of them starting to stretch, some of them listening in. "Did you see the starting roster?"

"See it?" Jerome said. His eyebrows furrowed. He grabbed a couple of cones and started out to the field to place them for drills and warm-ups. "I helped Coach B. create the roster."

"What?" Ethan asked, storming after Jerome. "And you let her put me on second string? On defense?"

Jerome laughed a little, his back still to him. "You weren't exactly performing at the last two practices, Ethan," he said. "You weren't even trying. Lots of guys want to play forward, and not too many wanted spots in the backfield, so you ended up there. And to be honest —"

Ethan didn't let him finish. He was so angry he could barely see straight. Before he could stop himself, he charged up behind Jerome and shoved him, almost knocking him down. The stack of cones tumbled to the turf.

When Jerome turned, Ethan could see he was ready for a fight. He shoved Ethan back but before

Ethan could throw a punch, Malik grabbed him by both arms and pulled him backward.

"Whoa, Ethan," Malik said.

Shaheed stepped in front of Jerome. "Save it for the game," he said.

Jerome angrily turned around and picked up a couple of cones. "Just keep him away from me," he said.

Ethan pulled out of Malik's grip and stomped to the sideline. He toed a ball out of the net bag and dribbled it toward the nearest goal, slamming it into the net. He needed to work out the anger bubbling up inside him. None of this was fair. Not one bit.

Has everyone gone crazy except me? He walked to the goal to get the ball again. *These guys were my friends and teammates last year.* Ethan took another shot, putting in all his frustration. *Now they act like I'm the bad guy. And the only thing that's changed is having Ms. B. as a coach.*

Malik walked up to the penalty area, almost directly in front of Ethan. "You cooled off?" he asked.

Ethan was still mad at Malik. But they were also still best friends. He kicked the ball to him. "Cool as I'm going to get," he said.

"Drills are starting," Malik said, knocking the ball back to Ethan.

"So?" Ethan said. "I don't really need drills. I'm not starting, remember?" He heard the tone in his voice and didn't exactly like it, but he really didn't like the current situation, either.

Malik shook his head and walked over to the cones where Jerome had already started the first drill.

Ethan fired one more angry shot into the goal and then walked over to join practice as it started.

CHAPTER 7

GETTING PICKED ON

Ethan went through the drills half-heartedly until, finally, Jerome passed out jerseys for a scrimmage. Ethan ended up on the red team and so did Malik.

In a scrimmage everyone started, since they needed to fill two teams. Malik, though, started at forward — Ethan started at D.

The sun was high enough already that the morning was hot. Ethan watched from the backfield as Sam took the kickoff and passed it to Malik.

Malik drove up the left side and passed it back to Sam at the top of the arc. Ethan could only watch as the two boys maneuvered past the other team's defense. He had to admit that Malik made a great assist, and Sam fired a great shot into the net's upper right corner.

The boys in red jerseys all cheered and clapped. "Nice shot, Sam," they called, or, "Great moves, Malik."

Ethan couldn't bring himself to cheer. He knew it wasn't very nice but he still felt too raw about everything. He jogged back to starting position and watched as the other team kicked off.

They started off up the right side. Jerome took the pass off center spot and dribbled upfield. He knocked a high pass over the midfielders to Shaheed, who took it to the left side — Ethan's territory.

Ethan closed on Shaheed but Shaheed spun and passed it to Javier, who was open at the top of the penalty area.

Ethan hurried after the ball to pick up Javier, but he snapped the ball right back to Shaheed, who had moved farther up the right side.

"Get on him, Ethan!" Malik called from center.

Ethan moved back toward Shaheed, but he didn't move as fast as he could have — he just didn't feel his normal fire for the game. Shaheed was able to slip past him and into the penalty area for a shot on goal.

The red team keeper hustled forward and with a nice dive just barely knocked the shot off course and out of bounds.

"Wake up, Ethan!" Sam yelled.

"What's the big deal?" Ethan turned on him. "They didn't score."

"Because Joshua made a great save," said Jerome, jogging over for the corner kick. "That doesn't mean you didn't drop the defense just now. You're not even trying. What is your deal?"

"I can't cover the whole backfield on my own," Ethan grumbled. He noticed that Malik was staring at him with a disbelieving look on his face.

Why is everyone picking on me today? Ethan thought as he jogged back to his position, fuming. He lined up with the others to block the kick but if he was unmotivated before, now he didn't care at all. If everyone was going to treat him like a sixth-grade scrub, what was the point in trying?

Ethan's team won the scrimmage, but when it was time to tell each other "good game" and give high fives, Ethan was already on his bike and riding home, wondering how the season he was so looking forward to kept getting worse and worse.

CHAPTER 8

UNFAIR

On Tuesday morning, Ethan was already at the front doors of Madison Middle School when one of the men from the janitorial staff arrived and unlocked the door.

"This is a first," the janitor said as he stooped in front of the door to unlock it. "In my twenty years working for this school district, I've never seen a kid so excited for a school day to start that he was waiting when I got here."

"I just need to talk to one of the teachers," Ethan said. "I'm not here because I love school so much."

The janitor swung the door open and held it for him. "Makes no difference to me," he said. "Long as you're not here to vandalize the place."

"I'm not, I promise," Ethan said. He hurried through the school to the science wing, found Ms. Brezinka's classroom door, and sat down to wait.

When she finally arrived, Ethan was pacing.

"Ethan Isaac," Ms. B. said as she unlocked her room. He moved to follow her in, but she blocked the door. "Sorry, Ethan. I have to prepare for the day."

"But I just —"

"Ah-ah," she said, cutting him off with one finger in the air. "Unless you're taking seventh-grade science again, my coaching office hours begin at three this afternoon — after school."

With that, she shut the door in his face.

* * *

Practice that afternoon began with two laps around the field. Ethan, though he was dressed for practice and on time, had decided he wasn't running.

"Mr. Isaac," Ms. B. said. She stood at the fence as he walked up to her, her clipboard hanging from one hand. "Why aren't you doing laps with the rest of the team?"

"I want to talk to you about the starting lineup," Ethan said.

"What about it?" Ms. Brezinka said. "Think someone's position isn't right?"

"Yeah," Ethan said. "Mine!"

"Ah." Ms. Brezinka nodded slowly. "Then this isn't about the lineup at all. This is about your ego."

"My what?" Ethan said. "No way. Look, I've been on the Muskrats for three years now, and I'm entitled — "

"Entitled?" Ms. Brezinka said, interrupting him. "I think feeling 'entitled' might be your problem. The only thing you're entitled to is a tryout and a free education. If you keep this up, you'll be lucky if Jerome and I let you warm the bench this season."

Ethan, his face hot with anger, said, "You just hate me because of science class last year."

"Mr. Isaac, is that what you really think?" Ms. Brezinka said.

"That's why you're giving me so much grief and that's why I'm not on the starting lineup! Just because I was lousy at science."

"Let me stop you right there," Ms. Brezinka said. "Your performance at tryouts hardly showed skills learned in two years of team play in middle school. You were lazy, disrespectful — of the game, your fellow players, and your coach — and you made it quite clear that you didn't plan to put your heart in the game."

"That's not true," Ethan said, even though he knew it was.

"And players with no heart," Ms. Brezinka went on, ignoring Ethan's comment, "don't start."

She glanced at her watch, blew her whistle, and waved over the team, who by now were finishing their second laps.

"The rest of the team is about to start position drills," Ms. B. said to Ethan without looking at him. "But you can go run your two laps — plus two more for starting late."

With that, she walked off to lead the rest of the team in their drills, leaving Ethan fuming yet again.

CHAPTER 9

THE FIGHT

The first opportunity for real play came from a pre-season game against the Hounds from Hamilton Middle School. Though the game didn't count for the season, it was a chance to see how the Muskrats could play against another team.

Ethan sat on the bench watching the starting Muskrat lineup get ready for the kickoff. Next to him sat a bunch of sixth- and seventh-graders and only one other eighth grader: the team manager, Emma Tzuck.

"I thought you'd be on the starting lineup this year, Ethan," Emma said.

"So did I," Ethan mumbled.

"You're disappointed," Emma said.

Ethan nodded and looked down.

"Coach Brezinka is disappointed, too. She told me." Emma said, her eyes open and honest.

Ethan thought about that for a moment. Disappointed about what? Disappointed she couldn't be meaner to him maybe. Except something in him knew that wasn't it. That irritating poke of guilt hit him again.

"She said you're wasting away your talent." She got up and put the clipboard down. She looked Ethan in the eyes. "I hope you stop doing that," she said as she walked away and checked the water cooler.

Ethan kicked the ground, trying hard to ignore Emma's words. Even though he knew she was right.

A few minutes later, the ball went out of bounds. Before the throw-in, Ms. B. stepped up to the bench. "Ready to play, Mr. Isaac?" she asked.

"Yeah," Ethan said.

"Alright." She waved for one of the backfield starters to get off the field. He headed for the sideline and Ethan got to his feet. Before Ethan could run in, though, Ms. B. stepped in front of him. "Show me some heart, Ethan."

"Yeah, I'll show you heart," he mumbled to himself as he jogged to his position, still smarting about Emma's comments. "I'm going to be the MVP of this game in a minute."

Ethan had only been in the game about thirty seconds when the Muskrats blew the drive. The Hounds moved quickly upfield.

"Here we go," Ethan said as he sprinted toward center.

"Watch your position, Isaac!" Ms. B. called from the sideline, but he hardly registered it. He didn't want to play defense anyway, and now was his chance to show everyone why he belonged up front.

The Hounds' striker moved to pass to their left wing, but Ethan intercepted the ball and drove across the center line.

"Clear it!" someone shouted from upfield. Ethan thought it sounded like Jerome. Another person yelled, "I'm open! Pass!"

Ethan ignored all of them and used some fancy footwork to get past two Hounds defenders. At the top of the penalty arc, he faked a pass to Malik, and then fired a shot at goal.

It went wide.

"Sub!" yelled Ms. B. She sent in another player. Ethan could hardly believe his ears. He'd gotten past a bunch of defenders and had even shot on goal — as a defender! And here he was being taken out of the game. He shook his head as he walked off the field.

"Ethan Isaac," Ms. B. said as he got to the sideline. "Sit on that bench, and get comfy. You're not playing again today."

* * *

Monday afternoon, Ethan, Malik, and a few of the other boys from the team sat down to eat lunch at the round table near the windows.

Ethan had survived the first week of practice and the first game, but barely. The cafeteria even seemed chilly thanks to the cold shoulder his friends at the table were giving him.

Also, he was still not a starter, and he and Ms. Brezinka still couldn't get along. And his mom had been giving him lectures every time she saw him.

He couldn't let it go. "Ms. B. just hates me, man," Ethan said right before taking a bite from his turkey sandwich.

"She doesn't hate you," Malik said. He struggled with the top of his milk before just setting it aside. "You hate her."

"Same thing," Ethan said, and the other boys at the table chuckled a little. "No, but for real. Ever since the first test in her class —"

"Which you failed because you didn't study," Malik pointed out.

Ethan didn't skip a beat. "— Ms. B. has had it in for me."

Malik shook his head.

"You know the worst thing?" Ethan said, leaning toward the other boys from the team — not Malik who was sincerely getting on his nerves. "She doesn't know anything about soccer."

Some of the other boys shook their heads. One rolled his eyes. What was wrong with everyone?

One of his mom's lectures rang through his ears. "If you knew how women often have to work twice as hard to be taken half as seriously as men, especially when it comes to sports . . ."

"Yeah, she does," Malik said. He finally had the top of his milk open, but it was torn a little.

He took a sip and some milk went down his chin. "First of all, she's been the girls' coach for like ten years."

"Eight years," Ethan corrected him. "And so what? What's it take to coach a bunch of girls kicking the ball all over the place and making sure their ponytails look good?" His ears burned. He didn't sincerely think that a girls' soccer team was like that. But he needed to make a point.

Malik shook his head at him again, looking disappointed in him.

"Like you should talk about good soccer, Ethan," said Joshua, the team's starting keeper. "I bet every girl on the soccer team knows not to go charging on goal from the backfield, ignoring her teammates."

"And ignoring the plays Coach has been going over at practice," Shaheed added.

Ethan laughed, but it wasn't a happy laugh. He couldn't believe they were all ganging up on him. "Maybe you should go play on the girls' team then," he said. "All y'all."

"Like that's an insult, Ethan. What's your problem?" Shaheed said. "Don't you have any respect for women and girls at all?"

His mom and dad had asked him the same thing. Ethan just crossed his arms and glared.

Joshua raised his eyebrows and nodded. "You should. Because you couldn't get through two minutes of Saturday's game without blowing it. The girls' team could play circles around you." He took a bit of his sandwich.

"And if Coach thinks you're being lazy," Malik added, "she's right. You barely try at practice."

"And you got milk on your chin," Ethan said, his voice hard even though he was trying to laugh it off. His whole body was tense.

Malik grabbed a napkin to wipe his face. "She and the girls' team got to the state semifinals last year," Malik said.

"So did we!" Ethan said. "With Mr. Levy as coach, remember him?" He hadn't known that about Ms. B., though. He wondered if, maybe, just possibly, he was wrong about anything else, too.

"Yeah, I do remember Coach Levy," Malik said, standing up and grabbing his tray. "And I wish I knew what he'd say to you to get you to shape up."

Ethan, his face growing hotter and hotter, said, "Maybe he'd say that he's glad I'm defending him."

"You're not defending him. You're defending your bad attitude. Grow up, Ethan," Malik said. He turned his back on the table.

"Hey, I figured it out, guys," Ethan said with a sarcastic edge to his voice. He felt like he did when he'd argued with his mom. Like the awful thing he was thinking just had to come out, even though a big part of him knew it was a bad idea and knew he was wrong. He said, "I guess you like Ms. B. because she's the only one who would be dumb enough to start you."

Malik turned around and slammed his tray back down on the table. He charged at Ethan.

Ethan pushed his chair back to stand, but it was too late. Malik knocked him to the floor.

Ethan tried to push him off, but Malik was a little bigger than him.

Mr. Trenchmire, the history teacher, pulled Malik off him, and as Ethan stood, someone grabbed him by the arms, too.

"Both of you," Mr. Trenchmire said. "Come with me. Time to see Vice Principal Paulsen."

They walked to the administrative office, neither Ethan nor Malik looking at each other. Mr. Trenchmire left them sitting side by side in wooden chairs in the lobby outside the vice principal's office. He asked the receptionist to keep an eye on them as they waited for Ms. Paulsen. Ethan leaned back and pulled at the torn spot on the knee of his jeans.

"I wish you'd knock it off," Malik said.

Ethan didn't look up. "Knock what off?" he asked, even though he knew exactly what Malik was talking about.

Malik sighed. "Fine," he said. "Go ahead. Keep giving attitude, playing like a jerk, talking smack about the coach all day. You can sit on the bench all season." He paused for a second and then said, "You know, I don't even know who you are right now."

Ethan's pang of guilt became an ache. Because at that point, he wasn't sure he knew who he was, either. He leaned back and crossed his arms and stared at the wall until Ms. Paulsen called them both in.

CHAPTER 10

COLD SHOULDERS

Malik completely ignored Ethan all day on Tuesday, from the bus to school, all during lunch, and then in the locker room before practice. The rest of the team just seemed irritated with him, either cracking mean jokes or hardly talking to him at all.

Just as bad, his parents were giving him the cold shoulder, too. Ms. Paulsen had called them and Malik's parents, assuring them that the next time there was a fight there would be a suspension. As it stood, Ethan and Malik had detention later in the week and Ethan's parents had grounded him indefinitely. Worse, though, was the disappointed look in his parents' eyes.

Running on the field now, Ethan tried to shake everything off. He figured the other players couldn't ignore him completely during practice. They had to run drills with him, after all.

The worst thing was: he was beginning to think they were right to be so standoffish. He was beginning to understand that his dislike of Ms. B. had more to do with him than her. And that maybe he hadn't been acting like the best teammate. Or person.

During a drill, Terrence almost knocked him over. "Oh, sorry," he said, backing away from Ethan. "Didn't know you were running drills. Didn't know you were on the team."

"Very funny," Ethan said.

For the scrimmage, Ethan put on a red jersey and took his position — on defense.

"Yo, Isaac," Jerome called from the center spot before he kicked off. "You sure you're in the right place?"

"Fullback," Ethan shouted back to him.

Jerome made a confused face. "No, isn't your position all over the place?" Everyone laughed.

Ms. Brezinka made a stern face. "All right, that's enough," she said. "Play ball."

But before long, Ethan missed the rude comments because instead everyone ignored him.

Jerome's team drove hard on the red goal, and Ethan picked up the defense. Jerome led the drive and passed to Malik. Malik passed across the penalty area to Preston. Ethan leaped in front of the pass and knocked it down. He recovered and went to clear the ball, but Preston snatched it back from him and knocked it across the field to Jerome, who'd gotten open.

Together, Preston, Malik, and Jerome maneuvered around the defense. Malik faked a shot and passed to Preston, who fired an easy goal before the keeper could recover from the fake. It was a new play, not one they'd used last year.

"Great job, boys," Ms. Brezinka said, clapping one hand against her clipboard. "Stuck to the play, and tight execution. Red keeper never saw it coming."

While Malik, Preston, and Jerome high fived and jogged back to the center line, Ethan stood stunned. It seemed Ms. Brezinka really did know her stuff. The team felt like a well-oiled machine. They worked together and knew what part they played — all of them. Except Ethan.

Because, Ethan realized, his heart dropping in his stomach, he had been a jerk.

Soccer was turning into science class all over again, with Ethan slacking off and not trying because it was a little hard. Worse, he was blaming the teacher again — this time, Coach — for his own issues.

Looking at his teammates, seeing how great they worked together, and how much they admired Ms. B., Ethan made a decision. Maybe, just maybe, he could start acting like the player and person he wanted to be.

CHAPTER 11

MAKING AMENDS

The next morning, Ethan paced in front of the red-brick face of Madison Middle School until the janitor strolled up with his huge key ring clipped to a retractable chain on his belt.

"You again," he said as he bent to unlock the door.

"Me again," Ethan said.

"Just another urgent conference with some teacher, huh?"

"With my soccer coach," Ethan said. And smiled to himself. He liked the way that sounded.

The janitor pushed the door open and held it for Ethan. "Good luck, then," he said.

"Thanks," Ethan replied, and as he took off down the hall toward the science wing, added, "I'm going to need it!"

When Ms. Brezinka arrived at her classroom in the science wing, Ethan was on his feet, waiting next to her door.

She saw Ethan and sighed. "Mr. Isaac," she said as she unlocked the door, "we've been over this. I keep my coaching office hours in my office near the gym. This is the science wing, so unless you have a science question . . ."

"I know," Ethan said. "I actually wanted to make an appointment to meet with you before practice, if you have time."

Ms. Brezinka swung open her classroom door and stood in the doorway a moment, looking at Ethan. She looked thoughtful. Finally, she said, "I have a meeting at 2:45, so let's say 3:15. All right?"

"Al lright," Ethan said. "Thanks." Relief swept through him. Maybe it wasn't too late to turn this around after all. He jogged to his locker, feeling hopeful for the first time in a long time.

It felt like the longest day of Ethan's life. At lunch, he got his tray and knew he couldn't sit with the guys from the soccer team. Not yet, anyway. Not until he'd made things right.

Ethan headed for a table in the middle of the room where he spotted Conner, Henry, and Philip, the boys who had quit the team at that first practice. The whole time they were eating, though, Ethan kept checking the clock.

"Yo, Ethan," Philip asked. "You got an appointment or something?"

"Yeah," Ethan said. "I need to talk to Ms. B. about the soccer team. I need to . . . make things better."

"What?" Conner said, making a face at him. "Who cares what she thinks, man? You should quit the team because you're a boy and that's the girls' team now."

The other boys laughed, but Ethan shook his head. "It's not like that," he said.

Conner snorted. "Oh, yeah? What is it like, then? You like playing on a girls' team?"

Ethan picked up his tray. For the first time since soccer started, Ethan was proud of his next move. He said, "First of all, why are you so afraid of girls? And second, I don't think most of us would make it on the girls' team, if you want to know the truth. Not if Ms. B. has been their coach for so long. She knows what she's talking about. You guys don't."

The three boys stared up at him, dumbfounded.

Ethan took his tray and threw away the rest of his lunch. He was too upset to eat. If he had sounded half as dumb as those three did . . .

He vowed to himself that he would make things better.

CHAPTER 12

A NEW PERSPECTIVE

"So," Ms. Brezinka said. She sat at her desk, tapping her pen. "Ethan Isaac. What can I do for you?"

"Well," Ethan said, trying not to feel the sweat run down his back. "Um." But he stopped and Ms. Brezinka motioned for him to sit in one of the chairs facing her desk.

He sat and tried again. "Well, after that game and after talking to Malik and . . . um, after practice . . . " Ethan felt stuck, not quite sure how to continue.

Ms. Brezinka said, "Go on."

He took a deep breath. "I haven't been a good teammate. I've been kind of . . . selfish and sort of weirded out . . " He looked down. He wasn't saying anything quite right.

"Weirded out by . . . ?" Ms. B. asked.

Ethan swallowed. "I guess . . . just because you're the coach?"

"Oh, am I?" she said, leaning forward, her elbows on the desk, a slight smile on her face. "I thought I was a science teacher."

"I mean, you're that, too," Ethan said.

Ms. Brezinka stood up and paced behind the desk to a small poster hanging on the wall. "Do you know what this is, Ethan?"

He stood and leaned across the desk to get a closer look. "It looks like an old photo of a girls' soccer team, Ms. B."

"Coach B.," she corrected, "and you're close, but at the college level, we call it 'women's soccer.' We don't use 'girls' soccer' any more."

"Right," Ethan said, sitting down again. "Sorry."

"That's all right," she went on, stepping even closer to the poster and squinting at the faces of the teammates, posed for a team photo.

"My parents couldn't afford to send me to college, so I was very lucky to have a scholarship." She turned from the poster and looked at him again. "They didn't give me a scholarship for my grades, that's for sure. My grades were terrible. My parents hardly spoke English, and I had a hard time keeping up in school when I was young. But you know what my dad loved more than anything — aside from" — she put on a strong Russian accent — "coming to America for opportunity?"

"Um," Ethan said, "soccer?"

Ms. Brezinka smiled. "That's right, Ethan," she said, sitting down at the desk again. "Soccer. He loves soccer, and I inherited that love from him. I've been playing longer than you've been alive," she said. "I got to go to college on an athletics scholarship because of soccer. I played on my college women's team all four years, and two of those years I was captain."

"Wow," Ethan said, genuinely impressed.

She nodded, seemingly pleased with the memory. "We went to the Division I semifinals my last year."

Ethan took another deep breath and felt his cheeks warm. "So. Yeah. You know what you're doing. I think I always knew that. Just, after doing so badly in your science class and needing extra help, I think I was embarrassed. So I fooled myself into thinking the problem was you and not me. Especially you being a girl and all — I just grabbed on to that because . . . well, it was the easiest thing to grab on to. I'm really sorry for the way I've acted."

"Thank you for saying so," the coach said. "I appreciate that. You know, in all my years of playing and coaching soccer, you're the first guy to ever apologize for his behavior."

"What do you mean?" Ethan said. "Do guys act like jerks a lot?"

Ms. Brezinka laughed. "Let's just say I've gotten used to guys thinking women's soccer isn't as tough as men's. That it isn't even a sport at all. The first time I heard some crack like that I was probably eleven years old, and they haven't really stopped."

Ethan looked at the photo on the wall behind her. Probably everyone in that photo heard stuff like that all the time, too, if Coach B. did. "I won't say stuff like that anymore. And I'll speak up when other guys do." He had a realization. "Like, Malik does." His admiration for his friend grew. Here he'd been so mad at Malik for not having his back. But all along he was doing the right thing.

"Thank you, Ethan," she said. "That means a lot." She smiled at him. "So, suit up. Practice starts soon. Remember, though: I want to see some heart. No more slacking."

Ethan grinned at her and nodded. He left the office and walked quickly to the locker room. He felt like something inside him had changed. Coach Brezinka had opened his eyes. Now it was time to prove that he deserved a spot on the team and to finally play the soccer he knew he could.

CHAPTER 13

TEAMWORK

At 3:45, Ethan was back in uniform and stretching against the fence before warm-up laps began. He felt energized.

Malik walked up to him, grabbing on to the fence. He said, "Hey, Ethan."

Ethan was thrilled he was there. He had some explaining to do. "Hey. I met with Ms. B. . . . I mean, Coach Brezinka today after school. I apologized to her."

Malik's eyes went wide. "Really?"

Ethan nodded. "Yeah. I think I've finally figured out that I've been a real jerk. To her and to you." He looked down and kicked at the ground a little. "You were right all along. And you stuck up for what was right this whole time. I'm really sorry. I promise I'm going to be a better teammate. And a better friend."

Malik looked at Ethan for a second and then clapped him on the shoulder. "You *were* being a jerk. But you're not now. I think I've finally got my best friend back." He grinned at Ethan and Ethan grinned back. He felt on top of the world. The two of them took to the track, running some warm-up laps and joking around like old times.

When Coach B. arrived, she gave Ethan a stern look and a small smile. It said to him, *Now's your chance to prove yourself.* And he intended to.

Coach jogged up to the boys on the field. "Scrimmage today," she announced. "Count off for teams."

The boys counted off until everyone had their teams. Ethan ended up on Jerome's team — he felt nervous but determined when he walked up to him carrying a red jersey.

"Here," Jerome said. "Coach B. says you're a midfielder now — attacking midfielder."

"Thanks," Ethan said.

Jerome answered. "It's totally her call. I still think you're an idiot."

Ethan said, "I don't blame you. I was an idiot. But that was then. This is now. I'm not going to let my team down again. I promise."

Jerome shrugged one shoulder, looking only a little surprised. "Just try not to mess it up for us, okay?" He turned and walked to the center line.

Ethan took a deep breath. This wasn't going to be easy.

* * *

The scrimmage took up the whole hour of practice, including a break to switch goals. The teams were evenly matched — neither one seemed to be able to score on the other team. Ethan had worked hard the whole scrimmage. By the second half, everyone was really feeling the miles they'd put on running up and down the field, but as attacking midfielder, Ethan felt it worse than most. He loved every minute, though — he was playing better than ever, making sure to support his team as best he could.

"Hustle, Ethan!" Jerome shouted to him as he cut across the center line for the hundredth time.

"Don't let him get in front of you, Mr. Isaac!" Coach B. called from the bench.

"Get it back to Jerome!" Terrence called from behind him as Ethan drove toward the penalty arc.

The sweat ran down Ethan's back but he made himself keep working hard. Late in the second half, he got the ball from the other team. Two defenders flanked him right away, but Ethan juked away from them. Normally, he would have tried for a run and a shot on goal, but out of the corner of his eye, he saw Jerome make a break. He dribbled around another defender and then made a strong pass to Jerome in the penalty area. Jerome out-maneuvered one defender and made a shot . . .

Goal!

His whole team went over to high five Jerome, Ethan included. He didn't even mind that no one gave him any pats on the back. He did what he was supposed to do and helped his team score. That was his reward. He glanced at Coach B. on the sideline. She gave him a thumbs up and he couldn't help but smile.

CHAPTER 14

PLAYING WITH HEART

The first official game of the season was that Saturday morning. It was a home game against the Cougars of Central Middle School, the same team that had beaten the Muskrats in the semis last year.

Ethan huddled with his team before the kickoff.

"First game," Jerome said, looking around the huddle. "We've got a good team, smart plays, and home field. We will win this game today."

The team grunted and hooted in agreement.

Jerome looked squarely at Ethan. "Ethan Isaac," he said, and everyone else in the huddle looked at him, too. "You're starting on the bench, but you're coming in to attack."

Ethan nodded. He was surprised but didn't say anything.

"Based on what we all saw at practice yesterday," Jerome continued, "you got a fresh start coming. Don't let us down."

Ethan set his jaw. "I won't," he said. And he meant it.

Jerome nodded. "All right, we break on three," he said to everyone, " 'Go Muskrats.' One, two, three . . ."

"Go Muskrats!"

Ethan joined the other second-stringers on the bench next to Emma.

"Coach B. took you off defense," Emma said. "You must be happy about that."

"Yeah," Ethan said. "Looking forward to getting out there today."

Emma leaned closer. "I'll tell you a secret," she said. "Coach B.'s putting you in. Five minutes."

Ethan leaned back and smiled. "Thanks."

Emma winked and sure enough, about four minutes into the game, the whistle blew and Coach Brezinka waved Ethan up from the bench.

"Shaheed," she called to the field as Ethan jogged up next to her, "take a seat."

Ethan ran out to his position as Shaheed jogged to the bench. They high fived as they passed. Ethan loved the feeling of being part of the team again. "Do it to it, bro," Shaheed said.

Ethan nodded and joined the game, determined to help his team. As attacking midfielder, he got into the action fast, rushing upfield with Jerome and Malik.

Malik had control of the ball and he drove upfield toward the Cougars' defense. As he reached them, he made a weak feint and passed it to the middle, where Ethan picked it up.

Jerome made a drive on his left and Ethan passed it to him. After reaching the ball, Jerome sent a high pass over the penalty area and Malik dropped it to the ground with a soft header.

Malik handled the ball across the box but the defenders swarmed him. He barely got a pass off back to Ethan. Ethan dribbled to the box's left corner, but got swarmed, too. He noticed Jerome open in the arc so he made a series of moves away from the other team and passed it to him.

Jerome drove two steps to the right, made a solid feint, and fired a shot left, sending the keeper sprawling to the grass . . . in the wrong direction.

The ref's arm went up for the goal. He blew the whistle and Ethan, Jerome, and Malik half hugged as they ran back to center spot.

"Great assist, Ethan," Malik said. He gave him a high five.

Jerome rubbed his head. "You're all right," he said, looking at Ethan from the corner of his eye. "Good handling, too. Seems like you're a part of this team after all."

Ethan smiled to himself as he hurried back to his starting position on the Muskrats' end of the field.

"Great first half," Coach Brezinka said when the boys were seated around the bench at halftime, drinking water and resting.

The score was one-all. Ethan had spent about ten minutes on the field in the first half and had one assist. He was tired, but not so tired that he wanted any more time on the bench today.

Coach Brezinka went over the first half with the players, offering critique where play fell apart and praise where play came together — like Ethan's assist for their only score.

To Ethan's surprise, she ended with, "Since Ethan seems to have finally joined the team, I think we should try him out starting in the second half. We'll put him at forward this half. All right with everyone?"

"Definitely," Jerome said. The other team members yelled yes — Malik the loudest.

When they were done, Ethan said, "You know it's all right with me!" A few guys laughed. Emma laughed, too, and patted him on the back.

The Cougars had kicked off to start the first half, so Jerome kicked off the second. He knocked the ball to Ethan, who took it across the center line and fired it back to Jerome. The defense closed in and Jerome turned and passed to Ethan.

Ethan drove up the middle toward the left side as Malik moved along the left sideline. Malik turned to lose his defender and was wide open when Ethan sent him a line drive pass.

Malik caught up to the ball and got control, then drove fast toward the box, passing to Jerome in the arc as he went. Ethan stayed behind Jerome to be there for a pass if he got swarmed. Sure enough, a moment later, Jerome was surrounded by defenders.

He turned and tried to pass to Ethan. One of the defenders tackled him, though, and took control of the ball, starting the Cougars' drive back upfield.

Ethan caught up with him. He cut in front of the Cougars' defender before he could clear, knocking the ball out of bounds. The ref blew the whistle and the Cougars took the throw-in from the sideline. Ethan dropped back on shallow defense on the right side.

With two minutes left in the game, it was still tied at one-all. The Cougars had control and their left wing took the ball up the sideline.

Terrence, playing right back, joined Malik to cut off the advance. When the Cougar passed to an open teammate in the center of the field — trying to get in front of the Muskrats' goal for an easy score — Terrence blocked it, knocking the ball to Ethan's position.

Ethan drove back to center and found Malik jockeying for position at the top of the box, with only his own defender and the Cougars' keeper between him and the goal.

Ethan passed high and long, counting on Malik's height to give him the advantage. Sure enough, Malik took the ball down with a soft header, got control, juked around his defender, and made a shot.

Goal!

Malik ran back toward center line, his arms up and a huge smile on his face.

"Awesome shot!" Ethan shouted, meeting him halfway.

"Great pass, Isaac," Malik said. "Turns out you know how to be a team player."

Ethan said, "It took me long enough," and the two boys grinned at each other.

He heard Coach B. yell from the sidelines, "Great job, Ethan and Malik!"

Ethan stopped running and gave his coach a thumbs up. She returned the gesture, making Ethan's grin even wider.

Ethan hustled back to his place on the team.

ABOUT THE AUTHOR

Eric Stevens lives in St. Paul, Minnesota. He is studying to become a middle school English teacher. Some of his favorite things include pizza, playing video games, watching cooking shows on TV, riding his bike, and trying new restaurants. Some of his least favorite things include olives and shoveling snow.

GLOSSARY

D (DEE)—short for "defense"

disbelieving (DIS-bee-lee-ving)—not thinking something is true

feint (FAINT)—a move that fakes someone out

indefinitely (in-DEF-uh-nit-lee)—not being clear or having a clear end

juke (JOOK)—a move that fakes out another player

pinny (PIN-ee)—another name for a mesh jersey used to distinguish one team from another during play

pre-season (PREE-see-suhn)—in sports, games or practices that happen before the official start of the season

rankled (RANK-uhld)—to be irritated or upset

scrimmage (SKRIM-ij)—a game played for practice

starter (START-uhr)—a player that begins on the field for sports games and often plays longer than those who don't start

DISCUSSION QUESTIONS

1. At the beginning of the story, Ethan really didn't want Coach B. to be his soccer coach. He said it was because she was a girl and girls shouldn't coach boys' soccer. Do you think there was a different reason he didn't want her as his coach?

2. Malik stood up for Coach B. and confronted Ethan about his behavior. Have you ever had to confront one of your friends about their bad behavior?

3. Ethan realized he hadn't been acting like part of the team. He expected to get a starting position without really trying. What does he do to make it up to his team? What does it mean to be a good team player?

WRITING PROMPTS

1. Write down what you would say to Conner, Philip, and Henry. How would you let them know that talking about girls and girls' soccer the way they did was not okay?

2. Ethan felt one way about Coach B. at the beginning of the book and felt a completely different way at the end of the book. Write a letter to Coach B. from Ethan's perspective at the beginning of the book. Then write a letter to Coach B. from Ethan's perspective at the end of the book.

3. What qualities do you think make the best soccer players and teammates? Write down a list of ten qualities good players seem to have.

More About
SOCCER

There are 11 players per team who play on the pitch during a soccer game. Different coaches use different player formations, or places where the coach thinks players should be. Below are some general positions in soccer:

Forward—the offensive players, often three of them, whose job it is to score goals

Striker—another name for a forward; sometimes referring to the center forward

Fullback—the defensive players, often three of them, whose job it is to defend the goal and are closest to the goalkeeper

Halfback/Midfielder—the players, often three of them, who make runs to score on goal but also run back to defend their own goal

Sweeper/Stopper—definitions vary. Often, these terms are used interchangeably for a player whose job it is to play on defense most of the time ahead of the fullbacks and behind the halfbacks.

Goalkeeper—the person who defends the goal. This position is the only one where the player can use their hands.

The field that soccer is played on is often called the "pitch."

The word "soccer" originated in Britain but now very few countries use the word. The vast majority of the world uses "football" to describe the sport.

The U.S. Men's National Team has yet to win a Men's World Cup tournament (there have been 20).

Soccer is played in over 200 countries worldwide.

The highest ever score in a soccer game was 149–0. A team was protesting bias in refereeing and scored 149 goals on their own goal.

The U.S. Women's National Team has won three Women's World Cup tournaments out of seven.